MEAN MACHINES

130   150

90

80

70

SUPERBOATS

PAUL HARRISON

ARCTURUS

First published in 2015 by Arcturus Publishing

Distributed by Black Rabbit Books.

P. O. Box 3263
Mankato
Minnesota MN 56002

Copyright © Arcturus Holdings Limited

Printed in China

Library of Congress Cataloging-in-Publication Data

Harrison, Paul, 1969-
 Superboats / Paul Harrison.
     pages cm -- (Mean machines)
 Includes index.
 Summary: "Describes fastest and biggest superboats including many facts, stats, and color photos"-- Provided by publisher.
 Audience: Grades K-3.
 ISBN 978-1-78404-076-5 (library binding)
 1. Ships--Juvenile literature. 2. Boats and boating--Juvenile literature. I. Title.
 VM150.H333 2015
 623.82--dc23

                              2014005062

Text: Paul Harrison
Editor: Joe Harris
Assistant editor: Frances Evans
Picture research: Mirco De Cet
Design: sprout.uk.com
Cover design: sprout.uk.com

Picture credits:
Ahmed Jadallah/Reuters/Corbis:4bl. Carlo Borlenghi/Alinghi/NewSport/Corbis:18tr. Crystal/Splash News/Corbis: 23c. Hovercraft Rentals, Orpington, UK: 20c, 21c. Incat/Buquebus Marketing: 16c, 17c. Innespace Productions Inc: cover c, 3br, 26tl, 26–27 bc, 27tr. Intermarine SpA, Messina, Italy: cover t, 28c, 29c, 29 inset. Limeydal:19c. PCN/Corbis: 18bl. Royal Caribbean Cruises Ltd: 12c, 13t, 13b. Shutterstock: 4–5 c (Iliuta Goean), 5tr (Geanina Bechea). SkySails GmbH: 30c, 31c. Ted Soqui/Corbis: 22c. U.S. Navy: cover b (Mass Communication Specialist 2nd Class Michael Smevog), 6t (John F. Williams), 6b (John F. Williams), 7c (John F. Williams), 14tl (Mass Communication Specialist 2nd Class Samantha Thorpe), 14b (courtesy of Northrop Grumman by Alan Radecki), 15 c (Mass Communication Specialist 2nd Class Michael Smevog), 24c (courtesy of Naval Sea Systems Command), 25tr (Photographer's Mate 2nd Class Sheldon Archie), 25bl (Courtesy of Lockheed Martin). Warby Motorsport: 10c, 11c.

SL004074US

Supplier 29, Date 0514, Print run 3419

CONTENTS

VICTORY TEAM OFFSHORE POWERBOAT

Class 1 offshore powerboats are the Formula 1 cars of the sea. They are designed to streak across water at speeds of more than 107 knots (198 km/h). Victory Team is one of the most successful competitors in this glamorous world. Their boats are really built for speed!

There are two seats inside the cockpit for the driver and "throttleman"—the person in charge of the boat's speed.

Two air intakes at the rear of the boat force air down over the engines to keep them cool.

These boats have two V12 engines—modified versions of the ones used in supercars.

Class 1 powerboat racing is the world's fastest water sport. Boats literally bounce across the seas at incredible speeds. But racing in these vehicles is crazily dangerous. Hitting the water at high speed is like hitting concrete, so the powerboat has to be super-tough. Even so, accidents and even deaths in powerboat racing are not uncommon.

Class 1 boats take a real hammering from the waves at high speed. The hull—the part of the boat in contact with the water—has to be both light and strong. Team Victory's hull is made of carbon fiber and Kevlar, which is also used to make bulletproof vests!

Entry into the cockpit is via a hatch in the roof of the boat.

The boat has two hulls, so it's called a catamaran. Two hulls can be quicker than one, because there is less drag.

SUPER STATS

VICTORY TEAM OFFSHORE POWERBOAT
TO SPEED: 137.6 knots (254.8 km/h)
POWERED BY: Two 8.2-liter V12 engines
ENGINE POWER: 850 hp
LENGTH: 40.6 feet (12.4 m)
WIDTH: 12.3 feet (3.750 m)
WEIGHT: 5.65 tons (4.95 tonnes)
MADE IN: Dubai

RV FLIP

If you're on board a boat and one end starts sinking into the sea, you're usually in big trouble—unless you're on the *FLIP* ship. This unique vessel is designed to tip up so it sticks upright out of the water. Most of the boat is underwater while the bulky bit at the back sits high and dry above the waves. It's all in the name of scientific research.

There is enough room on board for five crew members and 11 scientists—but it's a bit of a tight squeeze!

The furniture on board is attached to the walls with pivots called "trunnions." This means that the furniture spins around the right way up when RV FLIP goes vertical.

It takes about twenty minutes for the ship to go from horizontal to vertical.

The ship's design is based on the shape of a baseball bat—thin at one end and fat at the other.

To make FLIP *tip up*, the crew flood the ballast tanks in the thin part of the hull with water.

People on the boat have to brace themselves against the walls as the ship flips up.

FLIP stands for Floating Instrument Platform, and it's a scientific research vessel. A common problem for scientists studying the sea is that most boats bob up and down, messing up their calculations. That's not true of *RV FLIP*. So much of the ship is below the waves that it stays much more stable, and scientists can make accurate measurements.

FLIP *has no engines, so it has to be towed into its position.*

The scientific equipment is attached to three long arms called booms.

There is a machine on board that makes drinking water, so the crew never runs out—even on long excursions.

SUPER STATS

RV FLIP
MAXIMUM HEIGHT ABOVE WATER LEVEL:
   55 feet (17 m)
TOP SPEED: 7–10 knots
   (13–18.5 km/h) when towed
LENGTH: 354 feet (108 m)
WIDTH: 26 feet (7.93 m)
WEIGHT: 773 tons (711 tonnes)
MADE IN: USA

EARTHRACE / MY ADY GIL

Earthrace—later renamed *MY Ady Gil*—was a strange-looking superboat. However, its weird looks weren't just for show. Its strange fins and narrow hulls were built for a purpose—to make *Earthrace* a record-breaker and the fastest boat ever to sail around the world!

Three thin hulls allowed Earthrace to slice through the waves rather than have to travel over the top of them.

Earthrace *was made from carbon and Kevlar, two strong but very light materials.*

In 2008 Earthrace broke the record for the fastest boat to travel around the world. It *took 60 days, 23 hours, and 49 minutes to make the journey—* breaking the old record by 14 hours!

Conditions on the oceans can get pretty rough, so *Earthrace* was designed to survive waves up to 50 feet (15 m) high. She could also go up to 23 feet (7 m) underwater for very short periods.

Water on board the boat was recycled and any other liquids tipped overboard were thoroughly cleaned first.

Not only was *Earthrace* super-fast, it was also kind to the environment. This lean, green speed machine was designed to reuse, recycle or clean as much of the material used onboard as possible. Even the fuels and oils it used came from plants rather than traditional petrol or diesel. *Earthrace* was a superboat with a conscience.

In 2009, *Earthrace* was renamed MY Ady Gil (MY stands for motor yacht) and was used to monitor whale hunting.

In 2010, Ady Gil *sank after it collided with a whaling vessel.*

SUPER STATS

EARTHRACE / MY ADY GIL
TOP SPEED: 40 knots (74 km/h)
POWERED BY: Two biodiesel engines
ENGINE POWER: 1080 hp
LENGTH: 78 feet (24 m)
WIDTH: 26 feet (8 m)
WEIGHT: 28.7 tons (26 tonnes)
MADE IN: Australia

SPIRIT OF AUSTRALIA

Spirit of Australia is the most "super" of all superboats for one simple reason. It's the fastest boat EVER! If breaking the water speed record weren't a big enough achievement, what made it even more amazing was that *Spirit of Australia* was built in the owner's back yard using everyday tools and secondhand engines.

Spirit of Australia *is called a hydroplane. This type of boat is designed to skim across the top of the water.*

Water slows most boats down. However, hydroplanes are fast because water is forced downward by the bottom of the boat's hull.

The boat is made from timber and sheets of plywood—not the most hi-tech of materials, but clearly good enough!

There's just one seat to keep the weight down.

Spirit of Australia *is powered by a J34 jet engine, normally used in aircraft.*

Ken Warby bought his jet engines from the air force when they were selling off equipment they didn't need.

An Australian named Ken Warby designed, built, and drove *Spirit of Australia* by himself. He had no experience of building a boat like this but had always dreamed of breaking the record and was determined enough to succeed. *Spirit of Australia* broke the record on November 20, 1977. Convinced that his boat could do even better, Warby had another go in October 1978 and broke the record again. That record still stands to this day!

The Australian Royal Air Force helped out by giving the engine an overhaul before the record-breaking attempt.

The official world record was recorded at 317.6 mph (511.11 km/h)—but Spirit of Australia has hit quicker speeds.

SUPER STATS

SPIRIT OF AUSTRALIA
TOP SPEED: Up to 300 knots (555 km/h)
POWERED BY: J34 jet engine
ENGINE POWER: 1,587.6 lbs of thrust
LENGTH: 26.9 feet (8.22 m)
WIDTH: 8.2 feet (2.5 m)
WEIGHT: 1.66 tons (1.5 tonnes)
MADE IN: Australia

ALLURE OF THE SEAS

If biggest is best, then ships don't get any better than *Allure of the Seas*. This is the largest cruise liner in the world! It's like a floating city with shops, a 3-D movie theater, restaurants, a theater, an ice rink, and thousands of people on board. The ship is designed to give passengers the best time possible on the waves.

There is a park in the middle of the ship with 60 trees and thousands of other plants!

The ship has 16 passenger decks.

The bridge sticks out over the side of the hull so the crew can see the edge of the dock when it comes into port.

There are two climbing walls at the back of the ship.

There's even an old-fashioned merry-go-round on board!

At the back of the boat is a gigantic pool. It doubles as an aquatic theater and can spray more than 2,000 jets of water.

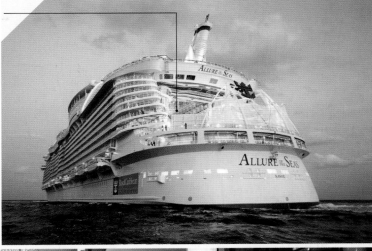

Cruise ships are like floating hotels, moving from port to port on grand sightseeing trips. *Allure of the Seas* travels around the Caribbean carrying more than 6,000 passengers. In addition, there are more than 2,000 crew members! You may think it would get crowded. Well, not on this ship—it's huge!

Many people think cruises are for old people. However, on the Allure there's a nightclub just for teenagers, scratch DJ lessons, and an automatic wave machine for surfing.

SUPER STATS

ALLURE OF THE SEAS
TOP SPEED: 22 knots (41 km/h)
POWERED BY: Four bow thrusters
ENGINE POWER: Four 7,500-hp engines
LENGTH: 1,187 feet (362 m)
WIDTH: 215 feet (66 m)
WEIGHT: 248,711 tons (225,282 tonnes)
MADE IN: Finland

You need a head for heights—the top of the ship is 213 feet (65 m) above the water line.

USS GEORGE H. W. BUSH

Aircraft carriers are massive warships that carry thousands of people and equipment for months at a time. The *USS George H. W. Bush* is the biggest warship ever made. If you could stand this ship on end it would be even taller than the Eiffel Tower. It's wider than six telephone poles laid end to end.

Being a warship means that the USS George H. W. Bush could find itself in some pretty dangerous situations. Parts of the ship's hull are protected by Kevlar to prevent damage.

Around 6,000 service personnel and crew live and work on board.

Even the windows have been specially toughened to withstand attack.

The George H. W. Bush usually carries 56 jet planes and 15 helicopters.

The ship was made up of 161 different sections, which were then joined together at the dock where it was made.

USS George H W Bush is part of the United States navy and it's a lot like a floating airport! The deck of the ship acts like the runway, the bridge is the control tower, and the aircraft are kept in hangars below the deck. But unlike normal airports, aircraft carriers like the *George H. W. Bush* can travel to wherever they are needed.

The deck is so big, you could fit three football fields on it!

Planes get an extra push when taking off from one of four catapults on the deck.

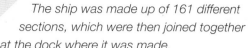

SUPER STATS

USS GEORGE H. W. BUSH
TOP SPEED: Around 30 knots (56 km/h)
POWERED BY: Four nuclear-powered steam turbines
ENGINE POWER: 280,160 hp
LENGTH: 1092 feet (332.85 m)
WIDTH: 257 feet (78.34 m)
WEIGHT: 100,153 tons (90,718 tonnes)
MADE IN: USA

Three strong wires, called arrester wires, are used to slow the planes when they land.

FRANCISCO

Francisco may well be the world's most exciting ferry. Most ferries lumber from one dock to another and then back again carrying passengers and usually their vehicles too. Not *Francisco* though—this is a super-ferry. It's actually the fastest ship on the water today—even quicker than most speedboats!

Francisco is classed as a ship rather than a boat because of its large size. However, it is much faster than most smaller crafts.

The ship is powered by two gas turbine engines, usually found on Boeing jet airliners.

Francisco can carry up to 1,024 passengers, plus 150 cars.

16

Francisco travels across the River Plate from Buenos Aires in Argentina to Montevideo in Uruguay. *Francisco* is so quick that it can compete with airlines over the 140-mile (225-km) distance between the two cities.

The ferry is named for Pope Francis, the head of the Catholic Church.

The catamaran design is used for stability and speed.

The hulls are made from aluminum.

Fuel is stored in the hulls of the ship—each hull provides the fuel for the engine on that side.

FRANCISCO

BUQUEBUS

SUPER STATS

FRANCISCO
TOP SPEED: 58.1 knots (107.6 km/h)
POWERED BY: Two gas turbine engines
ENGINE POWER: 2 x 59,000 hp
LENGTH: 324.8 feet (99 m)
WIDTH: 88.3 feet (26.94 m)
WEIGHT: 497 tons (450 tonnes)
MADE IN: Australia

USA 17

USA 17 was an extreme sailboat designed to race in the 2010 America's Cup. This is one of the oldest yacht races in the world, and pushes both the boats and their crews to their limits. This form of yacht racing demands an extreme superboat—and *USA 17* was that boat.

USA 17 *was a trimaran, which means it had three hulls.*

The three thin hulls were designed to slice through waves.

There were hydrofoils below the hulls to lift the USA 17 out of the water as it traveled, making it even faster.

USA 17 *was the fastest yacht ever to win the America's Cup.*

The USA 17's sails were rigid, a bit like a plane's wings. They were made from carbon fiber.

In 2010, sails were 190 feet (58 m) high—bigger than the wingspan of a Boeing 787 Dreamliner. They were later extended to a gigantic 68 m (223 feet)!

Although saiboats have been around for thousands of years, the *USA 17* was a very modern vessel. It had 250 sensors on board to measure everything from the wind speed to how fast the boat was traveling. This data was fed into a computer and was used to help improve the boat's performance during the race.

Usually, the rigid sails stayed up all the time—even on land. However, in strong winds they had to come down. This could take 24 people around two hours!

USA 17 needed a crew of 11 people to sail it.

The captain's sunglasses had a "head-up" display. This means information from the boat's computer would appear on his glasses for him to read.

SUPER STATS

USA 17
TOP SPEED: Over 40 knots (74 km/h)
POWERED BY: The wind!
ENGINE POWER: Not applicable
LENGTH: 112 feet (34 m)
WIDTH: 90 feet (27 m)
WEIGHT: 17.7 tons (16 tonnes)
MADE IN: USA

MEAN MACHINES

AV TIGER 12

How many boats can travel over land, water, mud, and even ice? Well, the *AV Tiger 12* can. That's because this superboat doesn't need to touch a surface. It travels over everything on a cushion of air. The *Tiger* is a hovercraft and, thanks to its unique way of getting around, it'll never leave you high and dry!

A motor below the boat blows a layer of air downward. The cushion of air is shaped by a thick rubber "skirt" at the bottom of the boat.

Originally, the Tiger was designed to carry 10 passengers.

There's space for two pilots at the front of the boat.

Rudders at the back of the boat behind the fans are used to steer the Tiger.

The huge fan at the back of the boat isn't for cooling passengers down, but for pushing the Tiger along.

The Tiger *is one of the quietest hovercrafts around—which is unusual, because normally hovercrafts are really noisy!*

The *Tiger 12* is a very useful kind of superboat. As it doesn't need water to move around, it is ideal for using in places such as mudflats or marshes. That's also why the *Tiger* has been used as a rescue vehicle—no matter where you're stuck, the *Tiger* will probably be able to come and help you!

Hovercrafts can't be used on really rough seas. That's because choppy waves make it too difficult for the "skirt" to keep the layer of air underneath the hovercraft in place.

GH 2126

The tube running around the boat at the top of the "skirt" is always filled with air. This stops the hovercraft sinking if air leaks out from the "skirt."

SUPER STATS

AV TIGER 12
TOP SPEED: 56 knots (104 km/h)
POWERED BY: 5.9 litre V8 engine
ENGINE POWER: 248 hp
LENGTH: 27.9 feet (8.53 m)
WIDTH: 12.5 feet (3.81 m)
WEIGHT: 3.3 tons (3 tonnes)
MADE IN: Great Britain

MEAN MACHINES

M/Y A

M/Y usually stands for motor yacht... but this luxury boat is more of a mega yacht! *M/Y A* took its styling ideas from stealth ships used in navies around the world. This superboat may not be the largest motor yacht on the water, but it is stunningly luxurious and has a unique appearance.. If you're rolling in money and want to stand out from the crowd, then this is the boat for you!

There is a crew of 42 people on board, split between those who sail the boat and those who look after the guests.

There are 14 guest cabins and a master suite.

The hull is made from steel.

A secret room is hidden away inside the boat, just for the owner.

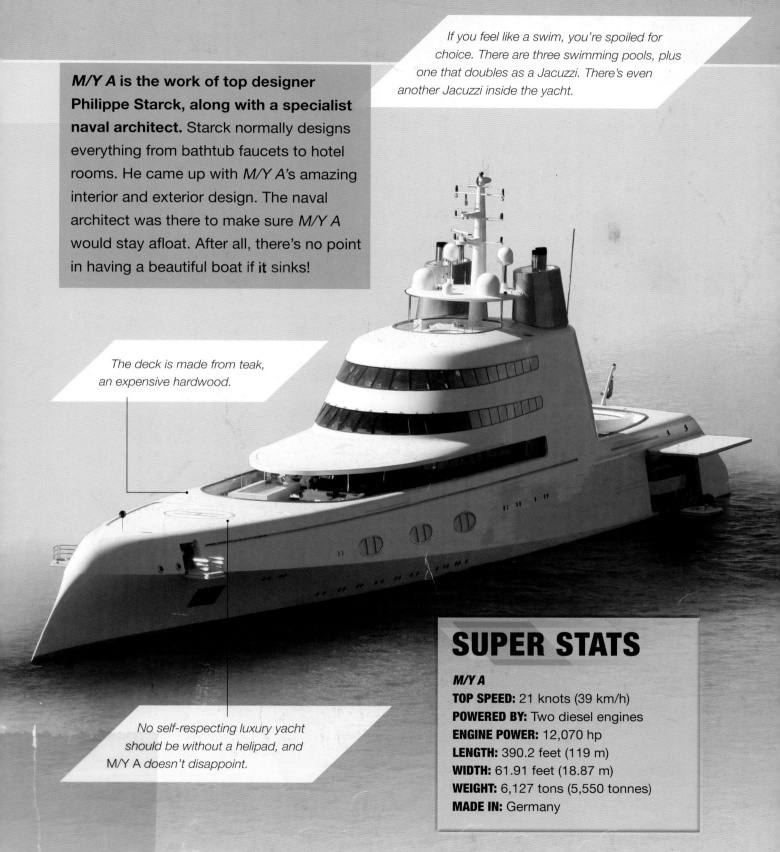

M/Y A is the work of top designer Philippe Starck, along with a specialist naval architect. Starck normally designs everything from bathtub faucets to hotel rooms. He came up with M/Y A's amazing interior and exterior design. The naval architect was there to make sure M/Y A would stay afloat. After all, there's no point in having a beautiful boat if it sinks!

If you feel like a swim, you're spoiled for choice. There are three swimming pools, plus one that doubles as a Jacuzzi. There's even another Jacuzzi inside the yacht.

The deck is made from teak, an expensive hardwood.

No self-respecting luxury yacht should be without a helipad, and M/Y A doesn't disappoint.

SUPER STATS

M/Y A
TOP SPEED: 21 knots (39 km/h)
POWERED BY: Two diesel engines
ENGINE POWER: 12,070 hp
LENGTH: 390.2 feet (119 m)
WIDTH: 61.91 feet (18.87 m)
WEIGHT: 6,127 tons (5,550 tonnes)
MADE IN: Germany

SEA SHADOW

If you spent around $240 million on a ship, wouldn't you want everyone to know about it? That wasn't the case with *Sea Shadow*. This special ship was a stealth craft designed for the US Navy. It used special technology that made it hard to detect—very handy if you're sneaking up on people!

The *Sea Shadow's* strange shape was deliberate. It made it difficult to detect with the radio waves used by radar.

The special black paint coating the hull also played a part in helping to hide it from radar.

The catamaran design helped the boat to stay stable on the waves.

There was space for 12 bunks on the ship, but there could be twice that number of sailors on board. It wasn't a squeeze, though—while one half of the crew slept the other was on duty.

The hull of the ship was at a 45° angle.

Sea Shadow was a top secret ship. It was never used in a conflict situation. Instead it was used by the US Navy to test out their stealth technologies. This ship was so secret that it was hidden away while it was being built and whenever it wasn't at sea. This, combined with its stealth capacities, made it unlikely that many people ever saw it at all!

For the boat to stay hidden, it was important for the hull to be as smooth as possible, so the door fit very snugly into the side.

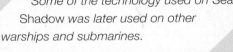

When the Navy had finished with their testing, Sea Shadow was sold for scrap. It was broken up in 2012! After all the money spent on the boat, the scrap price was just $2.8 million.

Some of the technology used on Sea Shadow was later used on other warships and submarines.

SUPER STATS

SEA SHADOW
TOP SPEED: 14 knots (26 km/h)
POWERED BY: 2 x diesel electric generators
ENGINE POWER: Top secret
LENGTH: 164 feet (50 m)
WIDTH: 68 feet (20.73 m)
WEIGHT: 618 tons (560 tonnes)
MADE IN: USA

SEABREACHER

Submarines may be exciting vehicles, but they tend to look a little bit... dull. Not *Seabreacher*, though—a super-submersible that can leap through the water like a dolphin and cut through the waves like a shark. Can there be a cooler way of traveling both above and below the water?

There are two seats: the pilot sits up front and the passenger behind.

It would cost you around $100,000 to buy a Seabreacher. That may seem expensive for splashing around in the water—but it's cheap compared to a luxury yacht!

The hull can be painted however the customer likes. Dolphin, shark, or killer whale designs are popular.

The interior of the Seabreacher can also be decorated however the customer chooses.

The *Seabreacher* isn't a true submarine. For a start, its engine needs air to work and it can't get air underwater. However, the *Seabreacher* can stay underwater for around a minute, so as long as you are happy to keep surfacing every now and again you'll be fine. It's a lot like being a dolphin!

A snorkel-like vent sends air to the engines.

The canopy is tinted, like sunglasses, to protect the driver and passenger from the sun's rays.

Cameras at the front and rear of the Seabreacher send pictures into the cabin.

SUPER STATS

SEABREACHER X
TOP SPEED: 43.4 knots (80.4 km/h)
POWERED BY: 1,500 cc supercharged engine
ENGINE POWER: 260 hp
LENGTH: 17 feet (5.18 m)
WIDTH: 3 feet (0.9 m)
WEIGHT: 1,350 pounds (612.35 kg)
MADE IN: USA

FSWH 37

The *FSWH 37* is a superboat with a difference—it "flies" across the water on underwater wings! The wings point down instead of pointing out to the side as on an aircraft. The *FSWH*'s wings do the same job as a plane's wings— they lift the boat up. And like a plane, the *FSWH* is super-fast!

The FSWH 37 *is used as a passenger ferry—probably for people in a hurry!*

The hull is made from lightweight aluminum. This material has the advantages of being strong and resistant to rust.

Underwater, the wings look like upside-down capital letter "T"s.

There's space for 250 passengers on board.

The *FSWH 37* is known as a hydrofoil. That's the name for a boat with wings (called "foils"). A hydrofoil uses its wings to make sure it stays out of the water as much as possible, so that there is less drag from the water. As the *FSWH* accelerates, the wings lift it up and the boat rises out of the water.

FSWH *stands for "Fully Submerged Wing Hydrofoil."*

Hydrofoils come in different designs. Some have wings that are partly visible on the surface. The main parts of FSWH 37's wings are completely underwater.

SUPER STATS

FSWH 37
TOP SPEED: 43 knots (80 km/h)
POWERED BY: 4 x 16V diesel engines
ENGINE POWER: 3,110 hp
LENGTH: 122.3 feet (37.3 m)
WIDTH: (26.2 feet) 8 m
WEIGHT: 33.1 tons (30 tonnes)
MADE IN: Italy

SKYSAILS

How do you turn an ordinary cargo ship into a vehicle at the cutting edge of green technology? Try adding a high-tech sail! You may have thought that the days of transporting goods on sailing ships were long gone, but think again. The SkySails system fitted to modern cargo ships shows that looking back to the past is the way forward for shipping.

The sail is around 3,445 square feet (320 sq m) in size.

The SkySail is controlled by a computer. It is released, controlled, and finally brought back on board the ship automatically, with very little help from the crew.

The kite flies up to 165 feet (50 m) above the ship.

The towing rope is 1,780 feet (421 m) long.

Ships that use less fuel don't just save money. They also cut back on the pollution in the Earth's atmosphere.

It might look too small to make much difference, but the SkySail can save a lot of fuel. It's also saving the ship owner's money by using the power of the wind to move the ship along. The main difference between the sailing ships of the past and the SkySails system is that these high-tech versions use old ideas in a brand-new way.

The SkySail is designed to help the ship's engines, not replace them.

The cable attaching the kite to the ship is made from a super-strong synthetic fiber. You don't want to lose your kite in the middle of the ocean.

SkySails can save up to 35% of a cargo ship's fuel cost.

SUPER STATS

SKYSAIL CARGO SHIP (THE STATS HERE ARE FOR THE *AGHIA MARINA*)

TOP SPEED: 14 knots (26 km/h)
POWERED BY: One diesel engine and a SkySail
ENGINE POWER: 8,000 hp
LENGTH: 557.7 feet (170 m)
WIDTH: 88.5 feet (27 m)
WEIGHT: 31,488 tons (28,522 tonnes)
SKYSAIL MADE IN: Germany

GLOSSARY

aluminum A silvery-white metal used to make lightweight products.

ballast tank An area within a boat that holds water and helps the ship float.

carbon fiber A thin, strong material made from rods of carbon. Carbon is also found in coal and diamonds.

catamaran A ship with two parallel hulls.

eco-friendly Not harmful to the environment

hovercraft A vehicle with an air-cushion that can travel on both land and water.

hydrofoil A boat that has fins, allowing it to lift off the water and travel at faster speeds.

Kevlar A man-made material that is very strong and resistant to heat.

plywood A strong type of board, made by gluing two or more layers of wood together.

radar A means of detecting objects using radio waves.

submersible A boat that can go underwater.

trimaran A ship with three parallel hulls.

trunnion A pin or pivot on which an object can be rotated.

FURTHER READING

Biggs, Brian. *Everything Goes by Sea*. Balzer & Bray, 2013.

Bowman, Chris. *Monster Ships*. Bellwether Media, 2014.

Graham, Ian. *Superboats (Designed for Success)*. Heinemann Library, 2008.

Hamilton, S. L. *America's Cup* (XTreme Races). ABDO & Daughters, 2013.

INDEX